# Nana's Place

Written by Akimi Gibson
Illustrated by Karen Meyer

SCHOLASTIC INC.

New York   Toronto   London   Auckland   Sydney

Copyright © 1994 by Scholastic Inc.
All rights reserved. Published by Scholastic Inc.
Printed in the U.S.A.
ISBN 0-590-27542-9

2 3 4 5 6 7 8 9 10          09          00 99 98 97 96 95 94

Jojo missed his Nana very much. She had been gone for a long time.

Jojo drew pictures of Nana. He made lists of the things she used to do. He even made a tall pile of her favorite records.

Jojo didn't want to forget Nana. But lately, it had been getting harder to remember everything about her.

"Jojo," Grandpa said, "Nana will always be with you."

"How?" asked Jojo.

Grandpa took Jojo for a walk. They went to Nana's garden.

"This was Nana's place," Grandpa said. "She loved being in her garden.  Take a good look around you, Jojo."

Jojo looked around very slowly.  He sat on the grass and closed his eyes.

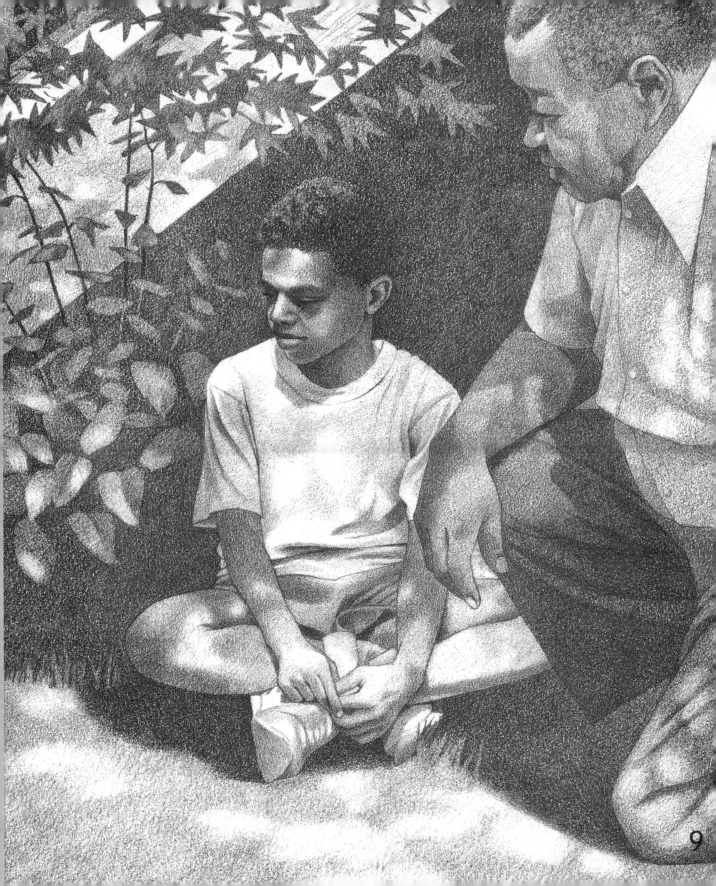

After a minute, Jojo took a deep breath. "Nana!" he yelled. "The garden smells like Nana!"

Jojo jumped up and ran to the patch of violets. "Look, Grandpa," he said, "purple was Nana's favorite color."

Just then Jojo stopped to listen to the birds. "The birds remind me of Nana's singing," he said. "Nana is everywhere!"

"That's right, Jojo," said
Grandpa. "Whenever you
want to remember your Nana,
come out to her garden.
Take in the smells, sights,
and sounds that your
Nana loved."

Jojo smiled as he sat in
Nana's place with Grandpa.
Together, they remembered Nana.